Care Bears

Snow Fun

SCHOLASTIC INC.

New York   Toronto   London   Auckland   Sydney
Mexico City   New Delhi   Hong Kong   Buenos Aires

ISBN-13: 978-0-545-01310-9
ISBN-10: 0-545-01310-0

12 11 10 9 8 7 6 5 4 3 2 1   7 8 9 10/0
Printed in the U.S.A.
First printing, December 2007
Designed by Michael Massen

Late one night, while the Care Bears slept, storm clouds passed over Care-a-lot. The air was cold and snowflakes swirled in the wind. Soon, all of Care-a-lot was hidden under a blanket of white snow.

Early that morning, Cheer Bear pushed off her covers
and rubbed the sleep out of her eyes.

"How beautiful!" cried Cheer Bear when she looked
outside. She put on her scarf, mittens, and boots.
Then she went to wake up her friends.

"Want to come out and play in the snow?" asked Cheer Bear.

"Sure, I'll put on my snow boots," said Friend Bear. "Let's go ask Surprise Bear to come along too!"

Cheer Bear, Friend Bear, and Surprise Bear headed for Grumpy's house.

Along the way they ran into some of their friends. All the Care Bears were planning a day of snow fun!

"I can't believe how much snow there is!" cried
Surprise Bear.

"We sure are lucky," said Good Luck Bear.

"It's perfect for sledding."

"I can't wait to go ice-skating," said Love-a-lot.

"Good morning, Grumpy," said Friend Bear.
"Want to come outside and play in the snow with us?" asked Cheer Bear.
"I'm too . . . sleepy," answered Grumpy Bear.

"Too sleepy?" asked Surprise Bear. "How could you be sleepy on a day like this?"

Grumpy didn't answer. Instead, he pulled the covers over his head.

"OK, Grumpy," said Friend Bear. "If you change your mind, come and find us."

When Grumpy Bear finally got out of bed, there was no one in sight.

It was very quiet outside. Too quiet.
Maybe I should go look for my friends,
Grumpy thought to himself.

Soon, Grumpy found a few Care Bears ice-skating on the pond.

"Wooah, wooah!" said Oopsy Bear as he tried to get his balance.

"Hey, Grumpy Bear," said Love-a-lot. "Want to skate with me?"

"No," said Grumpy Bear. "Skating looks too . . . slippery."

Grumpy trudged on through the snow and came to a hill. Some of his friends were sledding.

"Whee!" cried Laugh-a-lot as she and Good Luck Bear zoomed down the hill.

"Want to give it a try?" Funshine Bear asked.
"No," said Grumpy Bear. "That hill looks too . . .
steep."
Grumpy knew he didn't want to skate or sled.
But what *did* he want to do?

Next, Grumpy came across Tenderheart Bear, Bedtime Bear, and Wish Bear.

"Tenderheart, you made a beautiful snow Care Bear," said Wish Bear.

"Thank you," Tenderheart replied. "I like yours, too!"

"It's so cozy lying in the snow," said
Bedtime Bear, "I could almost fall asleep!"
Cozy? thought Grumpy Bear. *That snow
looks too . . . cold.*

Some of Grumpy's friends went inside to warm up and have lunch.

"I couldn't have wished for anything yummier than this hot cocoa," said Wish Bear.

"Come on, everybody! Let's get back out there! There is still a whole afternoon of snow fun to be had," said Champ Care Bear.

Grumpy Bear watched as his friends zipped down the slope.

"You can borrow my skis," offered Share Bear.

"No thanks," said Grumpy Bear. "Skiing looks too . . . fast."

Grumpy was feeling grumpier than usual.
He was the only one who wasn't having fun.
If only he could figure out what he wanted to do.

"Hey, Grumpy Bear!" called Surprise Bear.
"Do you like our snow bear?" Cheer Bear asked
with a smile. "We made it just for you."

"For me?" asked Grumpy Bear.
"You bet! We wanted to cheer you up,"
said Friend Bear.

"That snow bear looks . . . perfect!" said Grumpy.
Slowly, a smile spread across his face. "Can we
make another one together?" he asked.

"Of course," said Cheer Bear. "We were hoping
you'd join in the snow fun!"